Mrs. Jeepers'
Secret Cave

There are more books about the Bailey School Kids!

Mrs. Jeepers' Secret Cave

by Debbie Dadey
and
Marcia Thornton Jones

illustrated by John Steven Gurney

A
LITTLE APPLE
PAPERBACK

SCHOLASTIC INC.
New York   Toronto   London   Auckland   Sydney

ISBN 0-590-18981-6

12 11 10 9 8 7 6 5 4 3   8 9/9 0 1 2 3/0

Printed in the U.S.A.   40

First Scholastic printing, July 1998

Contents

Mrs. Jeepers' Secret Cave

1

Spelunking

"You'll never guess in a million years," Howie told his friends Melody, Eddie, and Liza. The four kids sat under the big oak tree on the school playground, eating ice cream.

"I guess you're trying to drive me crazy," Eddie said, licking his strawberry ice-cream cone.

"Don't be such a grouch," Liza told Eddie. "Howie is just trying to put some excitement into our summer."

"It's too hot to do anything fun," Melody admitted, pushing her black braids back before they got stuck in her ice cream. "This has been the hottest summer in the entire history of Bailey City. I can't wait for fall to come."

Eddie gagged on his ice cream, threw

1

his baseball cap at Melody, and pretended to die. "Don't even think such a horrible thing," Eddie said. "Cool weather can only mean one thing. School."

"I can't help it," Melody said. "When it's too hot to play, summer gets boring."

"Don't say that around my mother," Liza said. "Every time I'm bored she makes me clean something. So far I've washed the car and mopped the kitchen at least thirteen times."

Howie laughed. "I'm not talking about cleaning anything," he said.

"I know what we can do," Eddie suggested. "Let's go down to the library and throw water balloons at the statues. That will cool us off."

Howie put his hand on Eddie's shoulder and interrupted. "I'm not talking about causing trouble, either," Howie said.

"Then what are you talking about?" Melody asked.

2

"Exploring," Howie said with a smile.

Melody used her hand to fan her face. "It's too hot to explore."

"Besides, what's to explore around Bailey City?" Eddie asked.

"Someplace really cool," Howie told him, pulling a folded piece of paper out of his shorts pocket. "Ruby Cave."

Liza licked the ice cream that had dripped onto her hand and gulped. "Exploring a cave sounds dangerous to me," she said.

Eddie crunched the last of his ice-cream cone and talked with his mouth full. "You're a chicken. I think it sounds cool."

Howie laughed. "Actually, caves *are* cool. Even in the summer they never get very hot. It's so cold, we'll have to wear jackets."

"I still think it sounds scary," Liza said.

"It's not scary at all," Howie told her, opening the folded paper and holding it

4

up. The paper said: *Calling All Spelunkers to a Summer Adventure.*

"Spew-lunker." Eddie laughed. "That sounds like something used to fix the toilet."

Howie shook his head. "Spelunking is exploring a cave. I want you all to go with me."

"I don't know," Liza said. "Aren't there bats and creepy things like that in caves?"

"You ought to feel right at home since you're creepy, too," Eddie teased.

Howie ignored Eddie and handed the paper to Liza. "See," he said, pointing to the small print. "The camp is staffed by knowledgeable teachers and certified by the Bailey City Park Service. They don't certify just anybody. It has to be good."

Melody licked the last of her ice cream off her fingers. "Sounds fun to me. I'll do it."

"Well . . ." Liza hesitated.

5

"Don't be a chicken," Eddie said. "After all, what could happen in Ruby Cave with a teacher watching over you? I wish we could explore all by ourselves."

Liza's eyes got big. "You have to promise me you won't do that, Eddie. People have gotten lost in caves and they've never been found."

"You mean you'll do it if we promise to stay with the teacher?" Melody asked Liza.

Liza sighed. "I guess so, but I still think it's dangerous. I hope we don't regret this."

"We won't regret it," Howie said with a smile. "It will be the perfect summer adventure!"

2

Nightmare

Howie, Melody, Liza, and Eddie waved as Howie's dad drove away. Liza looked up the path leading to Ruby Cave. "I don't remember it being so steep," she said.

It was Saturday and Dr. Jones had driven the four friends to the foot of Ruby Mountain. They piled out of the car with their backpacks stuffed with everything they needed for their spelunking adventure.

"I remember this mountain," Melody said. "Especially Mr. Squash."

Liza's face got pale and Melody shivered as they thought about the strange man who had taught them how to square dance the last time they came to Ruby Mountain. They were sure he was a Bigfoot monster.

"Do you think Bigfoot is back?" Howie asked.

"I'm not afraid of Bigfoot," Eddie said with a laugh. "But I am afraid of Melody's big mouth!"

Melody curled her fingers in a fist and stuck it in front of Eddie's nose. "You better be afraid of me," she warned.

Howie stepped between his friends. "There are four of us and only one Bigfoot. We'll be safe."

"I hope you're right," Liza said in a tiny voice as she followed Howie up the steep path.

The four kids walked and walked. Even though the sun shone high in the sky, the path was covered in deep shadows from the tall trees. A bird screeched as they passed and Melody was sure she saw a shadow move.

"We're never going to make it," Liza whined when she stopped to catch her breath. "We've been climbing for hours."

"No, we haven't," Eddie said.

"How do you know?" Melody asked.

Eddie stuck out his arm so his friends could see. "My grandmother gave me this cool watch," he said. "I'll be able to tell you the time even when we're in the blackest part of the cave." Eddie showed off his new glow-in-the-dark watch. It was shaped like a bat, with jet-black wings and a face that glowed an eerie green.

"A bat watch is very appropriate,"

Melody said with a laugh, "since Eddie is batty. A bat brain!"

"It's appropriate," Howie said, "because caves are particularly batty."

"BATS?" Liza shrieked. "I don't want to spend the day with bats!"

"Don't worry," Howie said. "Most bats won't hurt you. In fact, bats are very helpful because they eat bugs."

"Are you sure?" Liza asked.

Howie stood up straight. "Have I ever been wrong before?"

"YES!" his three friends said all together.

Howie's freckled face turned as red as a strawberry. "Well, I am not wrong this time. We have nothing to worry about!" And then Howie continued stomping up the steep path.

Just as Liza was ready to give up, the four kids finally reached a clearing right next to the steep cliff of Ruby Mountain.

"We're here!" Melody called to Liza.

"Hooray!" Liza yelled.

Howie pointed to a small group of kids. "It looks like everybody else is ready to go. We'd better get over there so we can meet the spelunking expert."

Liza, Howie, Melody, and Eddie ran over to join the other kids standing in front of the black mouth of Ruby Cave.

"I can't see a thing," Eddie griped. He pushed his way to the front of the crowd. When he did, Eddie came face-to-face with his worst nightmare.

3

Cave Dust

Eddie took one look at his third-grade teacher and nearly fainted.

Mrs. Jeepers peered down at him with her flashing green eyes. She wore hiking boots, black jeans, and a sweatshirt. A polka-dotted bandanna around her neck was pinned with the big green brooch she always wore, and her long red hair was tied back with a green polka-dotted ribbon. Most kids at Bailey Elementary believed Mrs. Jeepers was a vampire and that the brooch was full of magic that made kids like Eddie behave.

"How very nice to see you," Mrs. Jeepers said in her Transylvanian accent.

Eddie's face turned white and he took a step back from Mrs. Jeepers. "What are you doing here?" he asked.

14

Mrs. Jeepers gently rubbed the green brooch at her throat. "I am your spelunking guide," she said. Then she smiled her odd little half smile. "I have spent many days exploring caves. I will enjoy guiding you deep into Ruby Cave so you may see how truly wonderful caves can be."

Melody gulped, and goose bumps covered Liza's arms. Eddie backed away when his teacher started talking to the rest of the kids. He didn't stop until he reached the shadow of a huge hemlock tree. He plopped down on the ground as Melody, Liza, and Howie joined him.

"This is summer vacation," Eddie moaned as if he were going to be sick. "We shouldn't have to see any teachers. There should be a law that teachers have to hide in basements during vacations."

Howie, Melody, and Liza fanned Eddie with their hands.

"It's even worse when our teacher might be a vampire," Liza whimpered, "and she's ready to lead us into a cave filled with bats."

"I bet Mrs. Jeepers is taking us to a bat reunion of vampires and we're going to be the main course at dinner!" Melody said with a gulp.

Liza nodded. "Vampires turn into bats, and bats hang out in deep, dark caves! What better place for a vampire to trap a group of innocent kids than in Ruby Cave?"

"I'm not exactly innocent," Eddie said. "And I'm definitely not scared."

"You're all being silly," Howie said. "Mrs. Jeepers is not going to serve us to her relatives on a silver tray with pickles and ketchup. She's just going to teach us about caves."

"It will be the last thing she teaches us," Melody said, "before she sucks our blood and leaves us as cave dust."

"We aren't going to end up as cave dust or bat bait," Howie told them. "This trip is perfectly safe."

"I'm not so sure we should go," Melody said. "Getting lost in a cave with the Queen of Vampires doesn't sound fun."

"Fine," Howie said slowly. "You can walk back down Ruby Mountain. Just watch out for Bigfoot."

Liza whimpered. "I don't know what's worse. Being lost in the woods with Bigfoot or following a vampire teacher into a cave."

"Well, you better make up your mind fast," Howie told her. "Because the rest of the group is getting ready to leave, and I'm going with them!"

"I've never let a teacher get in my way before," Eddie decided. "I'm not about to miss out on a chance to explore Ruby Cave."

"We'll be fine as long as we stick together," Howie added.

"I hope you're right," Melody said. "Or we may all be sorry!"

4

The Legend of Ruby Cave

"I can't believe we're going into Ruby Cave," a girl named Carey was saying when Liza, Eddie, Melody, and Howie joined the group of kids gathered by the cave entrance.

"I always wanted to explore Ruby Cave," Eddie said, "but I wasn't allowed."

A chubby boy named Huey nodded. "Nobody was allowed. It's been off-limits ever since my great-great-grandfather was a baby," he said.

"But the Park Service says it is safe," Liza interrupted.

Huey shrugged. "It wasn't always safe," he told the group in a low voice.

"What are you talking about?" Howie asked.

"The Bailey Bandits," Huey said.

"WHO?" Liza and Melody said at the same time.

"You've never heard of the Bailey Bandits?" Huey asked.

Howie and Eddie shook their heads.

Huey pulled the circle of friends close. "It was back in the days when stage-coaches traveled along the Sheldon Trail," Huey said in a low voice. "Old Man Bailey made his fortune mining gold during the California gold rush. He was bringing it home to Bailey City on the stagecoach. That's when the Bailey Bandits struck."

"What happened?" Liza asked.

Huey's eyes were big and round. "They robbed the stagecoach and took all of the gold!"

"Poor Mr. Bailey," Melody said. "I bet he was upset."

Eddie didn't look impressed. "What does any of that have to do with Ruby Cave?"

"When the sheriff and his posse

21

chased them, the bandits hid in Ruby Cave. The sheriff figured they were trapped, so he waited for the bandits to give up. They never did."

"What happened to them?" Liza asked.

Huey shook his head. "No one knows for sure. Legend says they never came out. Some people even believe the bandits' ghosts roam the cave to this very day, protecting Old Man Bailey's stolen gold! That's why nobody has been brave enough to explore the twisting trails of Ruby Cave. No one," Huey added, "until Mrs. Jeepers."

Suddenly, a shadow fell across the kids. They turned around to find Mrs. Jeepers towering above them.

"There is truth to the legend," Mrs. Jeepers said in her strange accent.

Eddie grinned. "You mean there really is a treasure?"

"And ghosts?" Liza whimpered.

Mrs. Jeepers smiled. "There is no need to fear ghosts," she said softly. "But caves hold dangers. It is easy to become lost in the darkness on the twisting paths."

"Aren't you afraid of the dark?" Melody asked.

Mrs. Jeepers shook her head. "I like the night, so the darker the cave the better. But be warned! You must follow the rules."

"Rules, rules, rules," Eddie griped. "Is that all teachers ever talk about?"

Mrs. Jeepers gently rubbed the green brooch at her throat and she flashed her green eyes in Eddie's direction. "Rules are for your safety."

"I want to be safe," Liza said. "What are the rules?"

Mrs. Jeepers looked each of the kids in the eyes before continuing. "There is only one. Stay with the guide."

"But that's you," Melody blurted.

Mrs. Jeepers smiled her odd little half smile. "Exactly," she said. "And my good friend Gordon. He shares my love of dark caves." Mrs. Jeepers waved her

hand toward a tall, thin, black-haired man. His hair curled up on either side of his head, reminding Liza of bat wings.

The man smiled, showing a huge mouth full of dazzling white teeth. He rubbed his long, thin hand through his hair. Mrs. Jeepers nodded to Gordon, and then she disappeared into the black mouth of Ruby Cave.

5

Living Cave

"We have to look for the gold," Eddie said.

"Not me," Melody said. "I'm staying with the guide."

"I want to go home," Liza whimpered.

"I don't think you have a choice!" Howie yelled as the other kids pushed Melody, Eddie, Liza, and Howie toward the black entrance of Ruby Cave.

"I don't like this," Liza said, sniffing.

"Don't get upset," Melody said, "or your nose will start bleeding." Liza's nose always started to bleed when she got too upset.

"There's no reason to worry," Howie said, patting Liza on the back. "We'll all be right here beside you."

"Yeah," Eddie said with a snicker. "Just

27

us, a Dracula teacher, a mad gang of ghost bandits, and maybe a few skeletons."

The kids grabbed flashlights from Gordon, then stepped carefully down the fifty damp steps leading to the cave floor. Every step led them farther into the darkness of the cave.

"Yuck," Liza said. "The wall feels slimy."

"That's monster blood," Eddie teased.

"It's just water," Howie told his friends. "This cave is alive."

"What?" Melody squealed.

Howie used his flashlight to point to the ceiling. "See where the water leaks in? That water has minerals and stuff in it that make the cave grow."

"That's a bunch of baloney," Eddie said. "That's not what was in our science book."

"I thought you never read that book," Liza said.

Eddie shrugged. "I looked at the pictures a few times and it said something

28

about living things needing to move and breathe."

Howie nodded his head. "That's usually true."

"Then this cave is as dead as a doornail," Eddie pointed out.

"But this cave is growing," Howie said. "I'm sure Mrs. Jeepers will tell us about it."

"Right before she sucks our blood out," Melody said with a nervous whisper as they came to the bottom of the steps.

Eddie laughed. "Yeah, Mrs. Jeepers and her batty friend, Gordon, will tell us everything. Did you see his weird hair? He looks like he's half bat!"

"Please," Liza begged. "If I have to be in this creepy place, at least don't talk about vampires."

"All right," Melody said. "No more vampire talk."

"How about ghosts?" Eddie said. "I think a Bailey Bandit just flew by me."

Liza grabbed Melody's arm and

squeezed tight. "Eddie," Melody warned. "Stop trying to scare Liza."

"Liza doesn't need any help," Eddie said. "All she has to do is look in a mirror and she'll scare herself."

"Shhh," Howie hissed. "Be quiet. This cave is known for its echoes. Everything you say loudly will echo."

"Cool," Eddie said, and before anyone could stop him he yelled, "LIZA IS A CHICKEN!"

The words bounced off the walls and came back at least ten times. LIZA IS A CHICKEN. LIZA IS A CHICKEN. Each time the echo got softer and softer until finally it disappeared.

"Children," Mrs. Jeepers said, "Eddie just demonstrated what *not* to do in a cave."

Eddie's face turned red and he looked at his dirty shoes.

"Please do not yell in the cave. Some of the rock formations could be loose. We do not want to have rocks sliding down on our heads," Mrs. Jeepers said with a smile. "I am certain it would be painful."

Melody jabbed her elbow into Eddie's side. "Not for Eddie," she said with a giggle. "His head is as hard as the rock walls of this cave."

"Now," said Mrs. Jeepers, "please stay close."

Liza gulped and squeezed Melody's arm tighter. "Ouch," Melody squealed. "Not that close!"

"Sorry," Liza apologized.

Mrs. Jeepers frowned and then continued. "Everyone must hold on to the safety rail and . . ."

Mrs. Jeepers paused to stare at Eddie, who was swinging back and forth under the safety rail. Eddie stopped swinging and stood up quickly.

Mrs. Jeepers continued, "And no one may leave the trail for any reason." Mrs. Jeepers turned and led them around a dark corner. The tiny electric lights that had been at the cave entrance were gone. The only light came from Mrs. Jeepers' and Gordon's lanterns, and the flashlights the kids carried.

"What would happen if our lights went out?" Liza asked nervously.

Melody shuddered. "Don't even think about it."

And then Melody, Howie, Liza, and Eddie followed their teacher into the deepest part of Ruby Cave.

6

Batting Around

"I'm tired," Liza complained. "We've been walking for hours."

Eddie checked his bat watch and shook his head. "No, we've been walking for exactly twenty bat wings."

Melody rolled her eyes. "How long is that in normal time?"

"Twenty minutes to ordinary people," Eddie said matter-of-factly.

"I don't think it's much farther," Howie told his friends.

"How do you know?" Melody asked.

Howie pointed to a big rock ahead of them. "There was a cave map in the registration packet. I studied it and I remember that rock comes before a rest point."

"I can't believe you study stuff in the summer," Eddie said. "That's scary."

"The shadows on these cave walls are what's scary," Liza said, waving her flashlight so it made crazy shapes on the walls.

Eddie put his hands together to make a hairy spider shadow. Liza took one look and screamed.

"It's all right," Melody told Liza. "It's only Eddie making pictures on the wall."

Liza groaned as she continued to walk the narrow trail. "I'd like to be home now, watching TV where it's safe and warm."

"Look," Howie said. "They don't have stuff like this on TV." He pointed his flashlight beside the rail. The trail dropped off into a huge cliff. Eddie kicked a pebble off the side and the kids listened as it bounced down, but they never heard it reach the bottom.

"No wonder Mrs. Jeepers told us to stay on the trail," Liza said with a gulp.

"One wrong step and we'd be potato peelings at the bottom of this cliff."

Eddie nodded his head. "We'd be four more ghosts roaming Ruby Cave."

Liza shuddered. "Don't talk about ghosts."

Eddie grinned. "How about ogres . . . or warlocks . . . or evil sorcerers?"

"Stop teasing Liza," Melody warned Eddie, "or I may have to turn you into a ghost myself."

"You guys are big babies," Eddie complained. "I was just trying to have some fun."

Mrs. Jeepers called from the beginning of the line of kids. "We are almost to Drakeburn Cavern."

"What is Drakeburn Cavern?" Melody asked.

Howie peered up ahead. "A cavern is a big room in the cave."

"I hope it's a bedroom," Liza said. "I need a nap."

"I think it's Mr. Drake's house," Eddie

teased. "He's waiting there to bite your neck." Eddie leaned toward Liza and pretended to bite her neck.

"Stop horsing around," Liza said. "It's too dangerous. Besides, we all know Mr. Drake left Bailey City. At least, I hope so."

Mr. Drake had been a school counselor at Bailey Elementary. He was very unusual and kept his office so dark that the kids believed he was really the king of vampires, Count Dracula.

"I wasn't horsing around," Eddie said. "I was batting around. Get it? I was a vampire bat."

"Here we are," Mrs. Jeepers said from up ahead. When the four kids caught up with her they found themselves in a huge underground room. Mrs. Jeepers lit several more lanterns that flooded the room with light.

"It's beautiful," Liza whispered. All around the children stood tall, pointy

columns of stone. The gold, orange, and red columns glistened and sparkled.

"It looks like ice-cream heaven," Eddie said.

Melody pointed to the cave's ceiling. Icicle-like columns of stone hung from the ceiling. "Whoever heard of ice cream stuck to the ceiling?" she asked.

The kids listened as Mrs. Jeepers explained about the rock formations. "Please do not touch any of the rocks in this room. One touch from you could kill them."

"See," Howie hissed to Eddie. "I told you this cave was alive."

"Yuck," Liza said. "I'd rather visit a dead cave."

Mrs. Jeepers rubbed her green brooch, frowned at the kids, and continued. "All the rocks here are called speleothems. They are made from dripping water that leaves trails of dissolved lime and other minerals. The rocks jutting up from the ground are called stalagmites. The rocks that hang from the ceiling are called sta-lactites."

"I never can remember that," Howie admitted.

Mrs. Jeepers pointed to a beautiful formation that looked like ice cream dripping from the ceiling. "An easy way to remember it is: Stalactites hold *tight* to the ceiling and stalagmites *might* grow tall enough to reach the ceiling. When stalactites and stalagmites join together, they are called columns."

Eddie pointed to a big round stalagmite that had a domelike top. "Hey, that rock looks like Principal Davis." All the kids laughed and looked around for rocks that looked like other people from their school.

"There are a few people I wish really would turn into rocks," Eddie whispered to Howie, "like Mrs. Jeepers."

"Don't wish that," Howie said. "If anything happened to Mrs. Jeepers or Gordon we'd be lost in this cave forever."

"Do you think Gordon knows this cave very well?" Liza asked.

Melody shrugged. "Mrs. Jeepers acted like he knew as much about caves as she did."

"But each cave is different," Howie told them. "Unless Gordon is familiar with this particular cave, he's as helpless as we are."

Eddie shivered. "Great. My whole life depends on a batty teacher who thinks my neck is an afternoon snack."

7

Frozen in Time

Liza pointed to a huge stalagmite. "Speaking of bloodsucking," she said. "That stalagmite looks like it could be a frozen vampire ready to attack." The stalagmite was as tall as Mrs. Jeepers but much fatter. It had a face with two long, sharp fangs, and a long flowing cape ending in jagged points.

"First it would have to do battle with that witch," Howie said, pointing to a stalactite hanging nearby. It looked exactly like a flying witch with long frizzy hair.

"Your pebble-sized brains are causing you to see things," Melody said. "I don't think they look like people. I think speleothems look like icicles, and this cavern reminds me of the North Pole."

"They look like long noses dripping

snot to me," Eddie said with a laugh. "And that reminds me of Huey."

Huey turned around and made a fist at Eddie, but Eddie pretended not to notice.

"All of these speleothems look like somebody," Howie said. "Those three in the corner look like skeletons." His three friends looked at the stalactites and stalagmites in the corner. They glowed eerily in the light from Mrs. Jeepers' lantern.

Eddie laughed. "That would explain what happened to those lost bandits in the Ruby Cave legend."

"That doesn't make any sense," Liza said.

"Sure it does," Eddie said, lowering his voice to a whisper. Howie, Melody, and Liza gathered close to hear. "Those bandits got lost in this cave and then turned into giant stone skeletons. I bet that's what's going to happen to us, too!"

"People can't be turned into stone," Melody said. "That would take magic."

"No one has that kind of magic," Howie added.

"Are you sure?" Eddie asked. He stared at Mrs. Jeepers at the front of the long line of spelunkers. The lantern she carried glinted off her green brooch as she pointed to a smooth glistening rock formation.

Melody giggled. "Eddie's right," she joked. "If Mrs. Jeepers has enough magic to make Eddie behave, then she would definitely be powerful enough to turn people into stone."

"Very funny," Eddie said. "I can see Mrs. Jeepers has already turned your brains to rocks!"

Melody was ready to whack Eddie, but Mrs. Jeepers started talking. "This is my favorite speleothem," Mrs. Jeepers said, pointing to a smooth glistening rock that looked as if it had oozed off a ledge.

Huey nodded. "That is a really cool sta-

lactite," he said. "It looks just like frosting on a cake!"

"This is not a stalactite," Mrs. Jeepers told him. "It is called a flowstone because flowing water caused it to form instead of dripping water. That is why it looks smooth like frosting. But," she warned, "if you tried to take a bite of this you would break a tooth!"

Eddie wasn't interested in learning any more about rocks. He wasn't interested in learning anything. "You sure know a lot about cave rocks," he interrupted.

Mrs. Jeepers smiled her odd little half smile. "Some of these rocks do seem like best friends," she admitted.

"How can a rock be a best friend?" Eddie asked. Then he reached out a hand to slap a nearby stalactite.

"STOP!" Mrs. Jeepers ordered, and her voiced echoed throughout the cave. Her hand flew to her throat and she gently rubbed the green brooch.

Eddie's hand froze. His glow-in-the-

dark bat watch hung in midair just
inches from the rock formation.

"Oh, no," Liza gasped. "Mrs. Jeepers
has turned Eddie to stone!"

8

Cave Monster

Eddie rolled his eyes. "I'm not turning into stone," he said, dropping his hand to his side. "I just didn't want to make Mrs. Jeepers mad at me."

"Please remember," Mrs. Jeepers said in her quiet Transylvanian accent. "These rocks are very sensitive. Touching them may destroy them."

"Gee," Liza said. "You make them sound like people who can get bruised skin and broken bones."

Mrs. Jeepers glanced at the rocks and smiled. "Perhaps they are a little like that," she said softly. Then she turned and led the kids farther into the cave.

"Did you hear that?" Liza said with a gulp. "She said they were like people. Eddie must be right."

"Think of what you're saying," Howie said.

"That the rocks are people?" Liza said.

"No," Howie said. "You're saying Eddie is right."

"Howie has a point," Melody said. "Eddie doesn't make a habit of being right."

"Hey," Eddie griped. "Just because I don't like three-digit multiplication problems, it doesn't mean I'm not smart. I have plenty of good ideas."

"Well, rock people isn't one of them," Howie said. "Now let's go before we get left behind."

Howie, Melody, Liza, and Eddie hurried after the rest of the kids. They followed Mrs. Jeepers down a dark passageway into another cavern. Eddie looked at his glow-in-the-dark bat watch and waved his arm in the air. "When are we going to eat?" he asked. "My watch says it's lunchtime."

Mrs. Jeepers acted as if she didn't hear.

She led the group out of the cavern and turned down another passageway. Where two tunnels met, she turned left and walked some more.

Eddie's stomach growled so loudly Melody heard it and giggled. "Eddie's stomach sounds like a cave monster," she said.

"It's not funny," Eddie said, looking at his watch. "It's past time for lunch."

"We have been walking for a long time," Liza said. "My legs are tired."

"Explorers have to be tough," Howie told his friends.

Melody nodded. "Maybe it won't be much longer," she added.

Melody was right. It wasn't long until the narrow passage opened into a huge cavern edged with glistening stalactites and stalagmites.

Mrs. Jeepers turned and smiled at the kids. "We will eat lunch here," she told them. "But remember, do not touch the speleothems."

Eddie, Melody, Howie, and Liza found a place to sit and opened their back-packs. They pulled out the sack lunches they'd brought. Eddie stuffed half of his peanut butter sandwich in his mouth all at once. Carey saw his puffy cheeks and giggled. Carey had a crush on Eddie, so she always giggled at him.

"Eddie looks like a cute little chip-munk," Carey said. Then she batted her eyelashes at Eddie.

Eddie opened his mouth and showed her his half-eaten peanut butter sand-wich. That was enough to get Carey to stop looking at him for a while. "I'd like to turn Carey into a cave skeleton," Eddie mumbled.

"Carey's not that bad," Liza said. "She just wants you to like her."

"I would like her a lot," Eddie admitted, "if only she'd move to an iceberg in Antarctica."

Just then, something darted between Eddie's legs. It was so pale, it blended in with the dusty ground. It skittered over a nearby rock and started climbing the wall.

Eddie jumped up and cupped his hands around it. "This is perfect," he told his friends.

"What is it?" Howie asked.

Eddie showed Howie the white salamander in his hands. Its long tail draped over his fingers and it took a few steps up Eddie's arm before stopping.

"It can't decide which way to go," Melody said.

"I can help it," Eddie said with a grin. Then he looked at Carey.

"You wouldn't dare," Liza said.

"Yes, he would," Melody said.

Before anyone could stop him, Eddie crept behind Carey and gently dropped the salamander on her shoulder. Then he hurried back to his friends.

Suddenly, a scream echoed throughout Ruby Cave and Carey ran straight to Mrs. Jeepers. Carey pointed at her own

shoulder and screamed again. "Get it off! Get it off!"

Mrs. Jeepers' eyes flashed in Eddie's direction, but she reached out her hand and scooped the salamander off Carey's shoulder.

"I'm surprised Carey screamed," Eddie said loud enough for everyone to hear. "I expected the salamander to scream when it saw Carey."

A few kids giggled, and some laughed out loud. Carey sniffed and gave Eddie her meanest look.

Mrs. Jeepers gently placed the startled creature on a nearby rock. "It could not see Carey," she said, "because it does not have eyes."

"No eyes?" Liza blurted.

Mrs. Jeepers nodded. "Cave dwellers do not need eyesight because they live in the comfort of darkness. They are called troglobites. Instead of good eyesight, they have excellent senses of smell and touch."

"Well, I don't have to have a great sense of smell to find the smelly cave monster in our group," Carey said, pointing at Eddie. "He's standing right there."

Eddie bowed, but most kids ignored him.

"Mrs. Jeepers, you really know a lot about caves," Howie said. "I didn't know animals could even live this deep in caves."

Mrs. Jeepers smiled. "The darkness of caves is appealing to many creatures," she said.

"I can't figure out how you even found this part of the cave," Liza said. "We took so many twists and turns it reminds me of a big maze."

Mrs. Jeepers nodded. "I could fly through these caverns," she told the group, "because I know them so well. But Liza has made an important point. Caves are not playgrounds. They can be very

dangerous. Never go into a cave alone, and you must always follow the directions," she said, "or else."

"What happens if you don't follow directions?" Liza asked.

Mrs. Jeepers didn't answer her. Instead, she stared straight at Eddie.

9

Cavern of Death

"You better watch your step," Howie warned Eddie.

"If you do anything else," Liza added, "you'll be in deep trouble."

It was after lunch and the group had continued following Mrs. Jeepers down another winding passageway.

Eddie stuck out his chest. "I'm not afraid of Mrs. Jeepers," he said.

"Well, I'm afraid," Liza said. "I'm scared I'll wear holes in my sneakers from all this walking."

"Where is Mrs. Jeepers taking us?" Melody said.

"There's only one reason Mrs. Jeepers is taking us farther and farther into the earth," Eddie told his friends. "To trap us."

"Don't be ridiculous," Melody said, but she didn't sound very sure.

"Think about it," Eddie said. Then he held up a finger and started counting. "First, Mrs. Jeepers is a teacher. It's a well-known fact that teachers don't want to spend their summers with kids. Second, she's on a friendly basis with rocks that look like glow-in-the-dark skeletons. Third, she's a vampire that enjoys sucking kids' blood through a straw. She probably brought Gordon along to help with leftovers. One, two, three. See, it all adds up."

Melody stared at Eddie before she finally rolled her eyes. "You *have* to start paying attention in math class," she said. "You are worse at adding than at spelling. Nothing you say adds up to anything."

"Sure it does," Eddie said, still holding up his fingers. "The only reason Mrs. Jeepers was willing to take us spelunking is so she could lead us straight into a

vampire trap. We're the main course in a vampire feast."

"I doubt Mrs. Jeepers would want you for dinner," Melody told Eddie. "You'd be too sour!"

Howie snapped his fingers. "I don't think Mrs. Jeepers is planning to snack on us," Howie said slowly. "But she may be up to something else."

"Like what?" Liza asked.

"Why would anybody spend an entire summer searching in an old cave," Howie said thoughtfully, "unless they were looking for the Bailey Bandits' treasure?"

"Do you really believe Mrs. Jeepers knows where the gold is?" Melody asked.

"The only way to find out," Howie said, "is to follow her." He shined his flashlight behind him. The light showed the black twisting passageway. "Besides, we'd never find our way back out of this maze by ourselves."

"Howie's right," Melody said. She looked up the passage. The last of the spelunkers had already disappeared around a bend. "If we don't hurry, we'll be trapped!"

The four friends rushed to catch up with the rest of the explorers. Liza zipped up her jacket and shivered. Howie stuffed his hands in his pockets. But Eddie had his jacket slung over his shoulder. "Aren't you cold?" Melody asked.

Eddie looked over his shoulder at Melody and nodded. "Sure I'm cold," he said. "But I figured Mrs. Jeepers and all her vampire friends would rather have a warm dinner. I'm letting my blood get good and cold so they won't pick me first."

Liza pulled her jacket up to her chin. "You better be kidding," she told Eddie.

Just then Mrs. Jeepers stopped and smiled back at the kids. "We are here," she told them before leading the kids into a huge cavern.

"Oh my gosh," Liza squealed.

"I've never seen anything like it," Melody whispered.

Howie nodded. "It's like a fairyland."

Eddie didn't say a word. He was too busy staring at the huge waterfall that stood before him. Water cascaded over golden rocks, and stalagmites and stalactites glistened all over the room. Everything sparkled as if covered with magical fairy dust.

"This is where we will enjoy snacks and this beautiful underground waterfall," Mrs. Jeepers said. "Then we must go back the way we came."

Gordon hurried to light several lanterns and the cavern flickered with warm light. His jet-black hair stuck up at the ends.

Most of the third-grade spelunkers slid their backpacks to the floor and dumped their flashlights inside. Howie slipped his flashlight in his pocket before sitting down to munch on a candy bar.

Liza raised her hand. "I remember the last big cave room was called Drakeburn Cavern. Does this waterfall room have a name?"

"The name of this room," Mrs. Jeepers said with a smile, "is the Cavern of Death."

Liza gulped and Melody gasped. Howie blurted out, "Why is this called the Cavern of Death?"

But Mrs. Jeepers didn't have a chance to answer because just then Huey pointed at the water. "Look!" he yelled. "There are fish in the water."

The kids hurried to look into the small stream that ran through the room. It was true. Tiny white fish swam in the water.

"Why do their eyes look so funny?" Liza asked.

"Maybe they saw you coming and glued them shut," Eddie teased.

Mrs. Jeepers shook her head. "No, these fish are blind," she told the kids. "Remember, it is dark in the cave without our lanterns and flashlights. They have no need for eyes."

"How did fish get all the way down here?" Liza asked.

"Most caves were formed by underground streams," Mrs. Jeepers explained.

Eddie pointed to the small trickle of water that made up the stream below the waterfall. "You mean that little bit of water made this huge cave?"

"At one time that little stream was probably a rushing river that hollowed out this cavern and all the other rooms in this cave," Gordon told him. "Parts of this cave are still being explored. Ruby Cave may even stretch under Bailey City."

"Yuck," Liza said. "You mean it might be under my house?"

Gordon nodded. "It's possible. Of course, Ruby Cave is nowhere near as long as a cave found in Kentucky. That cave is three hundred forty-eight miles long. Does anyone know what it is?"

Howie raised his hand. "Is it Mammoth Cave?"

"Very good," Gordon said, running his hand through his bat-wing hair. "Mam-

moth Cave is so big it has a restaurant called the Snowball Dining Room and regular bathrooms inside it. During one period of history, doctors used Mammoth Cave for a hospital, complete with hospital beds."

"A cave with beds sounds like my kind of cave," Melody said.

The rest of the third-graders were so busy listening to Gordon talk about Mammoth Cave that they didn't notice Mrs. Jeepers move all the way across the cavern. Howie was the only one who saw Mrs. Jeepers walk right up to a huge boulder.

"We've gone as far as we can go," Howie told his three friends. "This part of Ruby Cave must end at that boulder."

But Mrs. Jeepers didn't stop when she reached the boulder. Instead, she disappeared!

10

Mrs. Jeepers'
Secret Passage

"Did you see that?" Liza gasped.

"Mrs. Jeepers disappeared into thin air!" Melody whispered.

"No," Howie said. "She disappeared into a secret passage."

"We have to follow her," Eddie said.

"No, we don't," Liza blurted out. "I'm not about to follow a vampire teacher into a secret dark passage. She could be waiting there with all her batty relatives."

"But maybe she knows where the bandits' gold is," Eddie said. "I want some of that gold, too."

"Mrs. Jeepers said we should stay with the guide," Liza pointed out.

"Exactly," Eddie said. "And Mrs. Jeepers is the guide in charge of this adventure. I say we should go after her."

"Following Mrs. Jeepers *is* the only way to figure out what she's been doing in this cave all summer," Howie said, grabbing a nearby lantern. "We'll just have to make sure she doesn't know we're spying on her. We have to hurry before she gets too far ahead of us."

Howie checked to make sure no one else was watching. Then he sneaked to the rock wall and slipped in back of the same boulder that Mrs. Jeepers had disappeared behind.

Eddie pushed in front of Melody and Liza. "Howie better not find that gold before me," he said before disappearing into Mrs. Jeepers' secret passage.

Melody looked at Liza. "It's our turn," Melody said. Together, the two girls followed Eddie. The passage was so narrow, they had to walk sideways to fit through the crack. They held hands and slowly made their way through the tunnel. Liza was glad when they finally came to the end.

They found themselves standing in a small cavern, but Mrs. Jeepers was nowhere to be seen.

"That's weird," Melody said. "It would be pitch-black in here without Howie's lantern. How can Mrs. Jeepers see?"

"She's a vampire bat," Howie said solemnly. "She doesn't need light. She travels by sound."

"She must have gone around that huge column of rock on the other side of the cavern," Howie said. The column glowed in Howie's lantern light. It looked exactly like a huge skeleton grinning at the four trembling friends making their way across the cavern.

They were almost through the cavern when Liza tapped Melody on the shoulder. "Do you hear something?" she asked. "Or is my heart just beating really loud?"

Melody pulled on Eddie's shirt. "Slow

down," she hissed. "Liza hears something."

Eddie and Howie stopped walking so they could listen. "I hear it, too," Melody said.

Howie nodded. "It sounds like a deck of cards being shuffled."

"I think I know what that sound is," Eddie said slowly. His voice shook when he said it. Eddie pointed at the ceiling and Howie held up his lantern.

"THE CEILING IS ALIVE!" Liza screamed.

Howie, Liza, Melody, and Eddie stared at the ceiling, where thousands of bats hung upside down. A few had been flapping their wings, but at the sound of Liza's scream many more beat the air.

The four kids hurried to the far side of the cavern, as far away from the bats as they could get.

"It's a trap!" Eddie said. "Those bats knew we were coming."

"How?" Liza asked.

"Mrs. Jeepers called ahead using bat sonar, that's how," Eddie said.

"Eddie may have a point," Howie said slowly. "Bats use sonar to find their way around in the dark."

Liza gulped. "I just remembered what Mrs. Jeepers called this part of the cave," she said. "The Cavern of Death!"

"Let's not get carried away," Melody said. "After all, the bats aren't coming after us. They're still hanging from the ceiling."

Sure enough, the kids saw the bats in the light from Howie's lantern. A few flapped their wings, but that was all.

"Are you saying we should keep looking for Mrs. Jeepers?" Liza asked.

Eddie swallowed. "I think I just found her," he said.

Eddie pointed to a bunch of bats hanging right over their heads.

At that exact moment, Howie's lantern went out and the cave turned pitch-black.

11

Not a Sliver of Light

"We're going to be turned into stone skeletons!" Liza screamed into the darkness.

"Shhh," Melody hissed. "Not so loud. You don't want to start a bat avalanche."

"It's all right," Howie said. "My flashlight is in my pocket." Before Howie had a chance to turn it on, his flashlight clattered to the stone floor. Everybody dived for the ground to find it.

"I can't even see my hand in front of my face," Melody said.

There was not a sliver of light in the cave. Even on the darkest nights, Melody could see in her bedroom because there was a streetlight outside her window. But in Ruby Cave there were no streetlights, and there was absolutely no light.

"Ouch," Howie snapped. "Someone just grabbed my nose."

"Sorry," Liza said. "I thought it was the flashlight."

Eddie pulled his sleeve back and his bat watch glowed eerily in the darkness. It gave just enough light for Liza to see the flashlight lying on the ground. She grabbed it and clicked it on. The flashlight created a tiny circle of light around the group.

"Thank goodness we can see now," Liza said.

"I think I'd rather not see that," Melody said, pointing toward the ceiling.

Hundreds of bats filled the air above them. One bat flew dangerously close to Eddie.

"Take cover," Eddie screamed, and dived back on the ground. But that just made the bat dart closer to Eddie.

"Keep still," Liza warned. "They sense our movement."

Everyone was too scared to listen to Liza. They jumped around, causing the bats to fly close to their hair. Finally, everyone but Liza pulled their jackets up over their heads to hide. Liza sat perfectly still, shining the flashlight around her friends. With her eyes wide-open, she watched the bats swoop around and around, close to her. None of them dared fly into the tiny beam of light.

Mrs. Jeepers' voice cut through the darkness. "Do not be alarmed," she said softly.

Melody, Howie, and Eddie peeked out from under their jackets at the sound of their teacher's strange Transylvanian accent. Liza turned her flashlight beam toward the voice.

Mrs. Jeepers hung upside down from a rocky ledge, her long red hair streaming down toward the ground. She smiled

her odd little half smile before jumping down to the ground.

"My winged friends will not hurt you," she said. "They merely wish to be left alone." As Mrs. Jeepers spoke, the bats calmed their wings until they were perfectly still.

"How do you know they won't bother us?" Liza asked, her voice shaking.

Mrs. Jeepers smiled. "I have been studying this family of bats all summer," she explained. "This secret cave and its bats have been my special summer project. Now please follow me. We will leave these brothers and sisters to nap until evening."

"You mean you haven't been looking for the Bailey Bandits' treasure?" Eddie asked.

Mrs. Jeepers glanced at the bats clinging to the ceiling. "I did find a treasure here in Ruby Cave," she said. "These creatures are treasures to me."

"What were you doing hanging upside

down like a bat?" Howie asked Mrs. Jeepers.

Liza gasped. Was Mrs. Jeepers going to admit she was a vampire?

Mrs. Jeepers smiled her odd half smile and rubbed the green brooch. "To study bats in their environment, I needed to be 'batlike.' "

Melody gulped. In the tiny light from Liza's flashlight, Mrs. Jeepers seemed a little too batlike for comfort. Melody and Liza zipped their jacket collars up to their chins. Howie put his hands around his neck. Eddie just frowned. "Aren't you afraid you'll turn into a bat?" Eddie asked.

Mrs. Jeepers smiled again. "Would that be such a terrible thing? Bats are basically good creatures. After all, they eat bugs that pester people." And then Mrs. Jeepers turned and led the group toward her secret passage.

Mrs. Jeepers stopped just before leaving her secret cave. She pointed to a flat spot on the cave wall. Liza aimed her flashlight at the spot.

"Is it the Bailey Bandits' treasure?" Eddie asked.

Mrs. Jeepers shook her head. "It is a history treasure. Someone left a message from long, long ago."

The four kids huddled close to the wall. They could make out a faint red drawing on the rock wall.

"Wow!" Howie yelled. "Do you think cavemen did this?"

"Maybe the skeletons of the Bailey Bandits drew it with blood," Eddie blurted, "to tell us where they hid the treasure."

"Normal skeletons don't have blood," Melody pointed out.

Mrs. Jeepers flashed her green eyes at Eddie and Melody before turning and walking away.

"Nothing in Bailey City is normal," Liza whispered.

Eddie nodded. "Remember those spe-leothems?" he hissed. "I bet they really are the frozen skeletons of the Bailey Bandits. Mrs. Jeepers and her batty friends froze them when they were try-ing to escape from this bat cave."

"Don't be ridiculous," Howie said. "That would be impossible."

Eddie's friends glanced behind them while Liza swept the beam of her flash-light across the room. Sure enough, there wasn't a single speleothem.

"That's easy to explain," Howie said, but his voice didn't sound very sure. "There isn't any water dripping in here."

"That's it," Melody said with a trembling voice.

Liza shivered as she studied the cave drawing a little more. It looked more like a bear than a treasure chest to her. Still, the thought of skeletons in a cave of bats was enough to scare her.

Something must have frightened the bats, too, because at that exact moment, they fluttered their wings. "Let's get out of here," Liza squealed. "*Fast!*"

12

Mrs. Jeepers' Plot

The rest of the third-grade spelunkers were getting ready to hike back out of Ruby Cave when the four friends slipped back into the huge cavern. Mrs. Jeepers was standing off to the side, whispering to Gordon. They both stopped talking to look at Howie, Melody, Liza, and Eddie.

"It looks like Mrs. Jeepers and her batty friend are plotting something," Eddie said. Eddie would know. He was an expert at plotting trouble.

"What in the world would Mrs. Jeepers be planning?" Liza whispered.

Melody gulped. "Why are they looking at us?"

"I don't know," Howie said. "Unless . . ."

"Unless what?" Melody asked.

"Unless they're worried," Howie finished.

"Adults always worry when Eddie's around," Liza said matter-of-factly.

"I'm not just talking about Eddie," Howie said. "I'm talking about all of us."

"I wouldn't cause trouble," Melody said.

"But Mrs. Jeepers and Gordon don't know that," Howie said.

"You're not making any sense," Liza told her friend. "What kind of trouble could we possibly cause?"

"I know how to create a problem or two," Eddie said with a grin.

Howie shook his head. "You better not try anything. I think they're worried that we saw something," Howie said. "Something we shouldn't have seen in the bat cave."

"But we didn't see anything," Liza argued, "except bats and that animal picture."

"That's it!" Howie said. "If that picture

really is a code telling where the treasure is hidden, Mrs. Jeepers and Gordon could be worried we're going to go back there. We have to prove we're not going back."

"We have nothing to prove," Eddie said. "If that cave drawing tells us where treasure is, we'll have to go back."

Melody shook her head. "There's no way you're dragging me back into that cave with all those bats."

Howie grabbed his friend's arm. "Besides, we can't go back."

"Why not?" Eddie said. "We know the way to Mrs. Jeepers' secret cave."

"Because," Howie said, "I think I know Mrs. Jeepers' plot."

"What is it?" Liza asked.

"She's planning," Howie whispered, "to stop us!"

The four kids looked across the Cavern of Death. Mrs. Jeepers and Gordon weren't talking anymore. They were staring at Liza, Howie, Melody, and Eddie.

"I'm not afraid of them," Eddie said. He pulled free from Howie's arm and took a step back toward the secret passage. When he did, Mrs. Jeepers and Gordon started walking. And they headed straight for Eddie.

13

Hero

Mrs. Jeepers and Gordon moved so fast, they looked like they flew across the cavern floor. But they didn't move fast enough.

They were only halfway across the Cavern of Death when Carey darted between them and ran up to Eddie. She batted her long eyelashes at him and smiled. "Where have you been?" she asked. "It's almost time to leave."

Huey joined Carey just as Mrs. Jeepers and Gordon glided up to the group. "This has been a cool adventure," Huey told the group. "But I'm ready to get out of here."

Gordon looked straight into Eddie's eyes. "What about you?" he asked Eddie. "Are you ready to go?"

Melody crossed her fingers and Liza closed her eyes, but Howie spoke up before Eddie had a chance to answer.

"Of course we're ready," Howie said. "We've seen all there is to see."

Mrs. Jeepers smiled her odd little smile and spoke to Gordon. "I will lead the way," she said. Mrs. Jeepers turned and lined up the rest of the third-graders. Carey and Huey hurried away to be first in line. Then Mrs. Jeepers headed out of the Cavern of Death.

"Why did you answer for me?" Eddie griped.

"Because," Howie explained, "I didn't want them to think you were really going back to Mrs. Jeepers' secret cave."

"But that's where I want to go," Eddie argued. "It's the only way to find the treasure."

Melody tapped Eddie on the shoulder. "It's too late," she said. "The entire group is leaving. We have to go or we'll be left behind."

Eddie stomped his foot. "You've ruined everything," he complained.

"No," Liza said. "We've still had a great adventure."

"Yeah," Eddie snapped. "It's great if you like following a vampire teacher and her pal into a trap."

"Mrs. Jeepers didn't suck anybody's blood," Liza pointed out. "In fact, Mrs. Jeepers made sure we stayed safe. We really can't prove she and Gordon are vampires."

"Don't you think it's just a little bit weird that our teacher likes hanging out in caves?" Eddie asked his friends.

"That's not as strange as the bats calming down when they heard Mrs. Jeepers talk," Melody added.

"It's almost as if those bats recognized her voice," Howie said.

"If the bats know her voice, that can only mean one thing," Melody said. "She's one of them."

"I guess you're right," Liza said. "If it hadn't been for Eddie and his glow-in-the-dark watch we would have been their bat snack."

Eddie shook his head. "You were the brave one," Eddie admitted to Liza.

"You were the only one brave enough to shine the flashlight in the secret bat cave," Howie told her.

"Hurrah for Liza," Melody cheered, and it echoed throughout the Cavern of Death.

"You're a hero," Howie added. "That

means it's time for Eddie to stop calling you a chicken!"

Eddie's face turned red and he checked his glow-in-the-dark watch. "It means," he said, "that there's no time like a batty time in Mrs. Jeepers' secret cave."

"And I say it means it's time to get out of here!" Melody said. "Before we're turned into stone skeletons!"

"Do you really think those speleo-thems are the bandits' skeletons protecting a golden treasure?" Liza asked.

Melody, Howie, and Eddie looked at one another. "We'll never know," Howie said.

"There's one thing I am certain about," Melody finally said. "I'm ready to get out of Ruby Cave!"

Before they hurried out of the cavern, Liza stopped one last time to look at the glistening rocks and waterfall. "I never knew something so magical could exist near Bailey City," she said softly.

"You can be sure of one thing," Howie

said before turning and following the rest of the spelunkers out of the cave. "When you live in Bailey City, there's bound to be plenty of surprises!"

"And one of them," Melody added, "is Mrs. Jeepers' secret cave!"

Creepy Activities
and Puzzles

Ghost in a Cave Cookies

You will need a grown-up to help you with this recipe.

2 sticks of butter, softened
1 1/2 cups sugar
2 eggs
2 teaspoons vanilla extract
2 cups all-purpose flour
2/3 cup unsweetened cocoa
1 teaspoon baking soda
1/4 teaspoon salt
1/4 cup powdered sugar
red sprinkles

In a large bowl, beat butter, sugar, eggs, and vanilla together until fluffy. In a small bowl, mix flour, cocoa, baking soda, and salt, and then stir into butter mixture. Drop by rounded teaspoonfuls onto a cookie sheet. Flatten each ball of dough with a knife or a spatula. Bake for

8 to 10 minutes at 350°F. Let the cookies cool slightly, and then set on a plate.

Draw a ghost on a piece of waxed paper. Cut out the outline of the ghost on the waxed paper to make a stencil.

Place the waxed paper stencil on top of a cookie and gently shake the powdered sugar over the cookie.

Remove the stencil and give your ghost 2 red sprinkle eyes. Makes 4–5 dozen spookily delicious cookies!

Hidden Word Treasures

Can you find these words hidden in the cave? Words can be horizontal, vertical, diagonal, and even backward.

CAVE ✱ BATS ✱ EXPLORE
SUMMER ✱ RUBY MOUNTAIN
SPOOKY ✱ HAUNTED ✱ CAVERN
ROCKS ✱ TUNNELS

```
T A R E M M U S O R
U U V C O R C I K U
N O N T A P L H A B
M E U N R V Y A T Y
S P X A E T E U B M
P R U P E L X N A O
O A C Y L I S T X U
O S T A B O K E T N
K A U N V T R D U T
Y M O U N E X E R A
S R O C K S R I X I
A V E R U B L N E N
```

Answer on page 114

Hidden Bones

How many skeletons can you find in Gordon's office?

Answer on page 114

A Spooky Maze

Help this bat return to his cave, where the rest of his batty friends are hanging out!

Answer on page 114

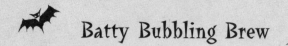

Batty Bubbling Brew

1 cup orange juice
3/4 cup cranberry juice
1/2 cup seltzer

Pour all ingredients into a container with a sealed top. Close the top and shake container. Pour into two glasses and enjoy this bubbling brew!

A String of Batty Friends

You need:

a piece of black construction paper
a pair of scissors
a pencil

Fold the paper in half.

Now fold the paper as if you were making a fan.

Trace the picture below and then cut carefully.

Hang your bats on your wall (upside down, of course!).

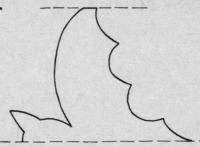

Monster Match

There are some weird grown-ups living in Bailey City! Can you match up these creatures with the names on the right?

Hercules   Nurse Redding

Bigfoot   Mr. Drake

Ghoul   Dr. Polly

Dracula   Mr. Belgrave

Cyclops   Scout

Gargoyle   Mr. Squash

Martian   Dr. Cerb

Skeleton   Mr. Stone

Answer on page 115

A Bone-good Crossword Puzzle!

Across

3. Where do the Bailey School Kids go spelunking?
5. Who tells the legend of Ruby Cave?
6. Some kids at Bailey Elementary think Mrs. Jeepers is a _____.
7. What color is Mrs. Jeepers' brooch?

Down

1. What time of year does this story take place?
2. What does Eddie have that glows in the dark?
4. A room in a cave is called a _____.

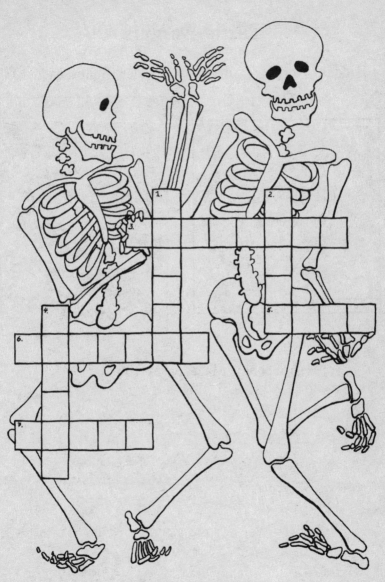

Answer on page 115

113

Puzzle Answers

Hidden Word Treasures page 104

Hidden Bones page 105

A Spooky Maze pages 106-107

Monster Match page 110

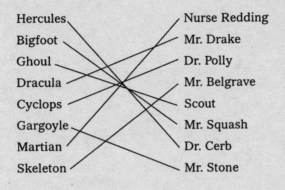

Hercules ─────── Nurse Redding
Bigfoot ─────── Mr. Drake
Ghoul ─────── Dr. Polly
Dracula ─────── Mr. Belgrave
Cyclops ─────── Scout
Gargoyle ─────── Mr. Squash
Martian ─────── Dr. Cerb
Skeleton ─────── Mr. Stone

A Bone-good Crossword Puzzle! pages 112-113

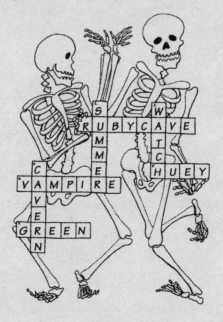

Debbie Dadey and Marcia Thornton Jones have fun writing stories together. When they both worked at an elementary school in Lexington, Kentucky, Debbie was the school librarian and Marcia was a teacher. During their lunch break in the school cafeteria, they came up with the idea of the Bailey School kids.

Recently Debbie and her family moved to Aurora, Illinois. Marcia and her husband still live in Kentucky, where she continues to teach. How do these authors still write together? They talk on the phone and use computers and fax machines!

Creepy, weird, wacky and funny things happen to the Bailey School Kids!™ Collect and read them all!

The Adventures of THE BAILEY SCHOOL KIDS®

❑ BAS43411-X	#1	Vampires Don't Wear Polka Dots	$2.99
❑ BAS44061-6	#2	Werewolves Don't Go to Summer Camp	$2.99
❑ BAS44477-8	#3	Santa Claus Doesn't Mop Floors	$2.99
❑ BAS44822-6	#4	Leprechauns Don't Play Basketball	$2.99
❑ BAS45854-X	#5	Ghosts Don't Eat Potato Chips	$2.99
❑ BAS47071-X	#6	Frankenstein Doesn't Plant Petunias	$2.99
❑ BAS47070-1	#7	Aliens Don't Wear Braces	$2.99
❑ BAS47297-6	#8	Genies Don't Ride Bicycles	$2.99
❑ BAS47298-4	#9	Pirates Don't Wear Pink Sunglasses	$2.99
❑ BAS48112-6	#10	Witches Don't Do Backflips	$2.99
❑ BAS48113-4	#11	Skeletons Don't Play Tubas	$2.99
❑ BAS48114-2	#12	Cupid Doesn't Flip Hamburgers	$2.99
❑ BAS48115-0	#13	Gremlins Don't Chew Bubble Gum	$2.99
❑ BAS22635-5	#14	Monsters Don't Scuba Dive	$2.99
❑ BAS22636-3	#15	Zombies Don't Play Soccer	$2.99
❑ BAS22638-X	#16	Dracula Doesn't Drink Lemonade	$2.99
❑ BAS22637-1	#17	Elves Don't Wear Hard Hats	$2.99
❑ BAS50960-8	#18	Martians Don't Take Temperatures	$2.99
❑ BAS50961-6	#19	Gargoyles Don't Drive School Buses	$2.99
❑ BAS50962-4	#20	Wizards Don't Need Computers	$2.99
❑ BAS22639-8	#21	Mummies Don't Coach Softball	$2.99
❑ BAS84886-0	#22	Cyclops Doesn't Roller-Skate	$2.99
❑ BAS84902-6	#23	Angels Don't Know Karate	$2.99
❑ BAS84904-2	#24	Dragons Don't Cook Pizza	$2.99
❑ BAS84905-0	#25	Bigfoot Doesn't Square Dance	$3.50
❑ BAS84906-9	#26	Mermaids Don't Run Track	$3.50
❑ BAS25701-3	#27	Bogeymen Don't Play Football	$3.50
❑ BAS25783-8	#28	Unicorns Don't Give Sleigh Rides	$3.50
❑ BAS25804-4	#29	Knights Don't Teach Piano	$3.50
❑ BAS25809-5	#30	Hercules Doesn't Pull Teeth	$3.50
❑ BAS25819-2	#31	Ghouls Don't Scoop Ice Cream	$3.50
❑ BAS99552-9		Bailey School Kids Joke Book	$3.50
❑ BAS88134-5		Bailey School Kids Super Special #1: Mrs. Jeepers Is Missing!	$4.99
❑ BAS21243-5		Bailey School Kids Super Special #2: Mrs. Jeepers' Batty Vacation	$4.99
❑ BAS11712-2		Bailey School Kids Super Special #3: Mrs. Jeepers' Secret Cave	$4.99

Available wherever you buy books, or use this order form

Scholastic Inc., P.O. Box 7502, Jefferson City, MO 65102

Please send me the books I have checked above. I am enclosing $_____ (please add $2.00 to cover shipping and handling). Send check or money order — no cash or C.O.D.s please.

Name_____

Address_____

City_____ State/Zip_____